Wild Wild Sunflower Child Anna

By the Same Author

Jesse Bear, What Will You Wear?

The Moon Came Too

Wild Wild Sunflower Child Anna

by Nancy White Carlstrom · illustrated by Jerry Pinkney

Macmillan Publishing Company New York · Collier Macmillan Publishers London

Macmillan Publishing Company
866 Third Avenue, New York, NY 10022
Collier Macmillan Canada, Inc.
Printed and bound in Japan
First American Edition

10 9 8 7 6 5 4 3 2 1

The text of this book is set in 16 pt. Garamond No. 3.
The illustrations are rendered in watercolor, gouache, and
colored pencil on paper and reproduced in full color.

Library of Congress Cataloging-in-Publication Data
Carlstrom, Nancy White.
Wild wild sunflower child Anna.
Summary: Spending a day outdoors, Anna revels
in the joys of sun, sky, grass, flowers, berries,
frogs, ants, and beetles.
[1. Nature – Fiction]   I. Pinkney, Jerry, ill.   II. Title.
PZ7.C21684Wi   1987   [E]   86-18226
ISBN 0-02-717360-7

For my husband, David,
Sher Smith, and Jane Yolen,
with love and thanks
—N.W.C.

In memory of
my mother,
Willie Mae
—J.P.

Running and jumping
silly and loud
is Anna
in the morning.
Wild wild sunflower child
Anna.

Flying in the field
in the greening
of the morning.
Anna drifts,
Anna glides,
Anna's arms open wide
for the sun rolling
sky falling.
It doesn't, Anna does.
Dizzy, tizzy Anna.

Digging in the garden
kneeling on her knees,
leaning on her elbows
whispering to the seeds.
Anna sifts the soil
lightly through her fingers.
Anna talking, Anna walking
sunshine.
Grow, grow
grow in the garden Anna.

Berries on the vine,
it's berry picking time.
Only ripe and juicy ones
that come off nice and easy.
Don't squeeze, Anna please.
Berry picking, berry licking
Anna.

Off goes berry nose Anna.
Skipping through
the snaggle bush,
slipping in her tangle rush.
Burr babies riding
on her shoulders,
burr babies sleeping
in her hair.
Anna Anna I don't care
Anna Anna burr baby
Anna Anna both feet bare.

Anna leaps
to the creek.
Hopping, hopping
rock to rock.
Great green frog eyes
bulging out at Anna.
Great green frog words
coming out of Anna.
Anna Anna begs
but frog doesn't answer
except for a frog splash
and that doesn't matter.
Tiny pools of water
trickle down Anna's legs.
Cool pool, trickle tickle Anna.

Anna climbs the hill
and keeps on climbing.
Up, up, up a tree
that turns into a ship.
Captain Anna stands on deck
sailing to a new world.
Brave, bold Anna.
High in the air,
tall please don't fall Anna.

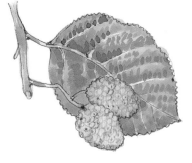

Anna Anna back to shore
Anna Anna back for more
dancing, dreaming
playing in the meadow.
Daisy chains
and Queen Anne's lace,
buttercup yellow
on Anna Flowerface.

Rolling Anna rolling
down the sweet smelling hill
Sky
    yard
        sky
           yard
Which will it be?
Anna Anna floating
on a grass green sea.
Prickly, stickly grasses
singing in her nose,
clinging to her yellow dress.
Green, fresh
oh what a mess Anna.

Wild wild sunflower child Anna.

Bending Anna bending
to the sunlight
and the shadow.
Passing ants
in their dance
pulling softly pulling.
Breathing in the gentle sounds
of rainbow color all around her.
Buzzing bees in purple clover,
Anna
        under
                Anna
                        over
Lifting up the pressing stone
beetles rushing giddy.
Spiders spinning silent webs
around the silver winking.
Silent spinning
buzzing, blinking
breathing rainbows Anna.

Swaying trees
blowing breeze
whistle kissing Anna.
Humming skies
closing eyes
golden flower lullabies.
Anna warm
Anna cradled
in the glowing
of the morning.

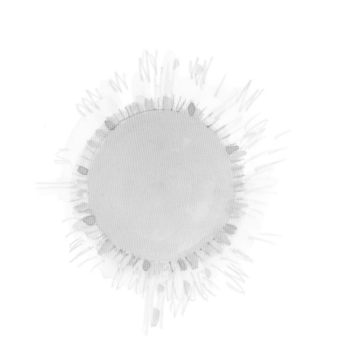

Sleep Anna
Sweet Anna
Wild wild sunflower child
Sleep.